The Lust Giving

Helen Walton

Walton House Publishing

Contents

A Short Story

♥

THE WARM SCENT OF pumpkin filled the kitchen. I loved pumpkin, even if it reminded me of a certain person and last Christmas. A person I'd see at dinner tonight. Nerves clenched my stomach, as I sighed.

I bent and retrieved the pumpkin pie from the oven. More of the delicious aroma drifted into the room. I smiled, happy with the pie but not the upcoming dinner. More importantly a certain guest.

At least the pie would please Emily. Her request was pumpkin pie, even though she preferred my banana caramel pie. I understood why she'd requested pumpkin instead since it was her brother's favorite.

Part of me wanted to deny her, but that's what best friends are for. It's why I couldn't say no to baking the pie for Emily's dinner, or to attending it.

The things we do for our longest childhood friends.

My phone buzzed with the song 'ABC' by the Jackson 5. Emily's joke when we'd celebrated her engagement with multiple glasses of champagne and ended up rather tipsy. The pie wobbled in my hand, like the champagne glass that night. I slid the dish onto the counter before I ruined dinner. It was a possibility anyway.

I shook off the oven mitts and snatched my phone from the counter.

"Claire," Emily whispered. "He's here already."

"Corn nuts," I mumbled, while my stomach twisted.

"Get over here now. He's grilling Jake. I told Travis way too much about Jake's life before we admitted our feelings and now it's coming back to bite me in the butt," she said with a grumble. "If only Natalie and

Conrad had been able to come too instead of spending Thanksgiving with his brother Tate and his girlfriend Olive. You're all I've got as a buffer, Claire."

"Okay, okay. I'll be there in a jiffy."

Hanging up the phone, I slid the mitts back on. I picked up the pie and made my way out the back door and hurried across the road to Emily's house. It used to be Emily's parent's house, but her parents and mine sold up and went traveling together. It was a no-brainer for either of us to buy our family homes even though she'd needed two roommates to make ends meet but look how well that had turned out for her now she was engaged to her roommate. Growing up as childhood friends living across the road from each other, we couldn't stand the notion of not living so close. Of not having our dream that our kids would grow up as best friends too. It appeared Emily would be the first to have kids. I didn't mind, or maybe I did. It put a hold on our dream when I no longer had a boyfriend and she was engaged.

Emily swung open her pristine white back door. "Quick, get in here," she hissed through clenched teeth.

I dashed into the equally pristine white kitchen. Emily shut the back door a bare second before the interior kitchen door swung open and Travis stood in the doorway. I froze with the pie in my hands, my gaze drinking in the sight of him.

"Thanks for getting the pie out of the oven," Emily gushed.

Travis surveyed the room, then narrowed his coffee-colored eyes. "Claire Bear."

His old nickname for me sent a tingle of closeness through my heart. And like that, my stupid crush was in full swing. Not my fault. Really, it wasn't. Travis was gorgeous, and not in an understated way. He could be a model with his high cheekbones, firm jaw, and brooding eyes under a decadent golden mane, but he was a famous actor instead, while my acting had gone nowhere and I'd ended up teaching drama in schools instead.

I stared up and up. He was almost a foot taller than me. It made me think about...nope, don't go there.

"Travis." I nodded. Proud of myself for sounding indifferent when my heart pounded inside my ribcage. See, I still acted well. He would never know how much he affected me with blinding lust.

His stare didn't waver. "I should've known you'd be coming to dinner too."

My mouth firmed into a tight line, and I returned his narrowed stare. So much for lusting after the jerk.

Emily rushed forward and slid her arm around my waist. "Of course, I invited Claire to dinner. She's part of the family. Where else would she be for Thanksgiving?"

Travis grunted and turned on his heel, letting the door swing shut in our faces.

"Man, he has a huge stick up his ass."

"Yep." I giggled. "It's a fine one, though."

Emily pinched my arm. "Hey, that's my brother."

"Sorry." Shit. How did I slip like that? I'd kept my crush on her brother a secret for so long. Why did I slip now? There was no way I'd ruin our friendship over Travis Campbell, actor extraordinaire, and A-grade corn nut. Not to mention the best kisser. Ever. I wouldn't tell Emily *that*.

Besides, the kiss was a lifetime ago.

Teenage hormones run rampant. Nothing more.

Except for dreaming on my part.

"Let's get this dinner over with." Then I'd go home and wallow in chocolate and ice cream and drown my feelings for Travis under a mountain of sugar.

I placed the pumpkin pie on the counter, shook off the oven mitts, and opened the kitchen door. In the dining room, Travis watched Emily's fiancé, Jake, across the round glass table. Jake appeared ready to throttle Travis with his bare fists.

"Hi, Jake." I sat at the table set with the special occasion plates decorated with gold leaves and sparkling silver cutlery. Emily was going all out to impress her brother. "How are you?"

"Good, thanks. And you?" Jake tugged on the collar of his white shirt, then ran his hand through his hair.

"The kids ran me ragged this week. They were all excited about the volleyball clinic on the beach. I got a little too much sun filling in for the physical education teacher."

"You always had a nice tan," Travis said. "Wine?"

I swung to my right. Did Travis compliment me? I nodded mutely as my heart pounded. Travis poured a good measure of red wine into my sparkling wine glass and Emily's too.

"You do," Emily said, carrying a large serving dish into the dining room. "I envied your tan growing up. Travis and I lucked out with the pale skin."

"I like your pale skin."

Did I say that?

Heat traveled up my neck to my cheeks. Lucky for me, the color wouldn't show on my bronzed skin, not like when Emily blushed.

"Are you still working at Westerly Elementary School?" Travis asked.

"Yes." I sipped my wine. "Are you still filming in England?"

Could this get any more awkward? I shouldn't have come to dinner. My palms grew damp. I should have made the pie and told Emily to collect it. Travis was right, I wasn't family, and I'd never be a member of their family. Disappointment sat heavy in my heart.

Travis reached for the serving spoon. "No. I'm moving back here for a franchise of films."

"You are," squealed Emily.

"I am." He nodded and filled his plate with the delicious smelling creamy mashed potatoes. "You cooked all the favorites like Mom used to."

"It's not every day you're here for Thanksgiving. If I'd known this was a homecoming dinner, I would've made something more extravagant."

My eyebrows rose of their own accord. Emily cook something more extravagant? She didn't even cook dinner tonight.

"I wanted to surprise you. When you told me you were engaged, I figured it was time to come home before you have kids." He ate a forkful of pasta. "I can't let you and Claire corrupt my future niece or nephew."

"Corrupt?" I frowned. "The way I see it…" I bit my tongue and tasted the metallic tang of blood.

"The way you see what?" Emily asked, her long hair swinging as she looked my way.

"Nothing." I stretched for the serving spoon.

Travis turned the handle of the spoon my way. Our fingers brushed. Awareness shot down my arm. Even after all these years, my body still flared from his touch. I gazed at Travis's lips. Why did they have to be so delicious?

Jake cleared his throat. I slopped a spoonful of mashed potatoes onto my plate and handed him the spoon with no awkward hand touching. I dug into the turkey. It was better to keep my mouth full of food rather than say anything to Travis again or gaze at his lips in longing.

"There won't be kids yet," Emily said around a mouthful of food. "We're not ready for babies."

"It's what all newlyweds say." Travis waved his fork. "Before you know it, there'll be one, then two, then three little mini Emily's and Jake's running around."

Jake tugged on his shirt collar again. "Emily's right. We're not ready for kids. We're both busy filming the sitcom."

"Then why are you getting married?"

Jake's mouth flapped. Could Travis be any blunter? Emily swirled her mashed potatoes around her plate. It didn't look like she would say anything either. Guess it was up to me.

"Because, Travis, when two people are in love, they get married. It doesn't have to be about the white picket fence and two-point-three kids, the dog and cat, the minivan, and all that jazz." My blood heated with my outburst.

Travis frowned. "Is that what you want, Claire?"

"What?" I spluttered. "Me?" I wanted it all. Everything I said. A husband, a family, a sense of belonging, and being needed by those I loved and who loved me.

"Yes, you. You are engaged to Kevin."

"Not anymore. I broke up with him."

"Emily didn't mention your breakup. When did this happen?" He placed his fork on the table and eyeballed his sister in question.

Emily rolled her shoulders.

"After Christmas last year." I swallowed.

The Christmas Travis had brought his English model girlfriend, Nina, home for Christmas dinner with both families before our parents left for their trip. Travis and I usually avoided each other, but this time we couldn't. Nina was stunning in her beauty, smart, and as tall as Travis. A perfect match. I was jealous. So ridiculously jealous I'd broken my engagement to Kevin, knowing he deserved better from his future wife. More so after the way Travis and I helped

Emily in the kitchen with the cooking, where we'd talked and laughed like old times, and reconnected in a way I'd always wanted.

"About time you dumped the sleazeball." He picked up his fork and ate more of his meal.

"Sleazeball?"

"Travis don't," Emily muttered.

"What's going on?" I swung my head back and forth between the two siblings.

"I walked in on him hitting on Nina."

"Kevin hit on Nina?" My stomach dropped.

"Yes. Wasn't the first time, from what I hear." He scraped the last of his turkey and stuffing with his fork.

Humiliation scorched a trail through my body. I'd always known Kevin was a flirt, but I'd assumed it was harmless and his natural personality that he'd never cheat on me. Now I wasn't sure.

I picked up my half-eaten plate of food, stood, and said, "I'll get dessert."

Fleeing to the kitchen before my emotions took hold. The door opened and Emily followed me into the kitchen, carrying the rest of the plates I'd left on the dinner table in my haste to escape.

"Are you okay?"

"Sure, why wouldn't I be? I realized Kevin was a flirt." I smoothed my damp palms down my lemon-yellow dress. "Tell me, did he cheat on me?"

"No," Emily said. "Wasn't his flirting the reason you broke up with him?"

"Yeah, sure," I said, moving to the pumpkin pie. Let Emily assume Kevin's flirting was the reason and not my crush on her brother. How long did a crush last, anyway? Lusting after her brother hadn't gotten me anywhere in all these years, so why would it matter?

I shoved through the door and carried the pie to the dinner table.

"Looks delicious, Emily," Jake said.

I placed the pie in the middle of the table and kept up the pretense Emily was the one who'd baked the pie. I didn't mind.

She wanted to prove to Travis she could cook after the fiasco with Christmas dinner where Travis and I ended up in the kitchen, together, alone, and...

Emily sliced pieces of pie for everyone.

"A perfect pastry." Travis lifted his plate and examined his piece of the pie. "Let's see if your pie tastes as good as it looks, Emily."

"You can be such a food snob," Emily said.

Travis shrugged and slid his fork into the pie.

I held my breath. Funny how I longed for his approval. The pumpkin pie disappeared into Travis's mouth. Through his delicious lips. I couldn't tear my gaze away. He licked a dab of pie from the corner of his lips. What I wouldn't give to be that morsel of food. I rolled my eyes at myself. Now I was jealous of pie.

I shook my head and turned my attention to my piece of the pumpkin pie.

"This is excellent, Emily," Travis said.

"Sure is," I agreed. "Great job with dinner tonight."

Travis's lips twitched.

"Thanks." Emily tucked her hair behind her ear.

Travis scraped his plate clean. "You could always become a chef."

"Definitely not. I love my job." She squeezed Jake's hand. "And now I get to act every day with the love of my life."

"I'm proud of you for getting the sitcom role."

Emily eyeballed me. I tapped the corner of my lips. Our code for keeping a secret. I wouldn't tell Travis I was the one who cooked the pie. It would be Emily's and my little secret. Like Travis's and my secret kiss. My lips were not letting those secrets spill to the other.

"How's your girlfriend?" I asked, changing the subject, not because I wanted to know. It was the last thing I wanted to hear, Travis with his perfect model girlfriend.

"We broke up." Travis waved his hand with a shooing motion.

Did he shoo his model girlfriend away? I ate more pie before I laughed because his words caused giddy happiness to take up residence in my heart. Travis was single.

"Didn't either of you want to do the long-distance relationship?" I asked.

"Actually, we broke up months ago, before New Year's."

"Emily didn't tell me."

My heart stuttered. Stopped. Started beating with a frantic rhythm. Did our moment in the kitchen at Christmas mean something to Travis, too? Or was I the only one who imagined there was more to it? With trembling fingers, I fumbled for my wineglass and knocked it over.

"Corn nuts. Sorry." I jumped up and patted the table with the napkin, but I was too slow, and the red wine made a perilous path toward Travis's lap. The liquid rolled and dripped from the edge of the table. I pressed my hand on Travis's lap and dabbed at the mess. Dab dab. Dab dab. My hand worked overtime, eager to clean up my mistake.

Travis grabbed my arm. His warm fingers were tantalizing around my frantic pulse. I paused and gazed into his eyes. It wouldn't take much to...

Jake laughed. Emily giggled.

"OMG!" Heat filled my face. What was I doing? Dabbing at Travis's lap like a crazy person. A crazy, infatuated person. I dropped the napkin on the table and slunk down in my seat. See? Dinner ruined.

"All right, you two," Emily said. "Out with it."

I snapped my gaze to hers and avoided looking at Travis.

"What are you talking about?" Travis asked with forced laziness.

Emily huffed. "I saw you two kiss."

"We didn't kiss at Christmas," we said in unison.

Emily's mouth fell open, closed, opened. She gawked at me, then Travis, then back to me. Emily narrowed her eyes the same way Travis did upon seeing me. She swung back to Travis. "I meant the year we had the lemonade stand. You two left to get more lemons, and you were gone so long that I went looking and found you kissing."

"Oh, that," I whispered. So many emotions churned in my stomach.

"Yes, that." Emily swung back to me. "Why didn't you tell me? We're best friends and tell each other everything."

I gulped, and said, "I couldn't tell you, because I didn't want to lose you."

Emily leaned forward and squeezed my hand. "You'd never lose me."

I turned my hand over and squeezed back. "I'm sorry, I should have told you."

"Yes, you should have told me years ago when it happened."

"Why are you bringing it up now?"

"Because I know you, and I know Travis. I've seen the looks you give each other. You're both single and living in the same city again." She smirked. "I figured it was time to clear the air before you sneak around behind my back."

Shaking my head, I said, "I wouldn't do that to you."

"I know. That's why I'm saying this here and now with you two in the same room. I can't believe it took my engagement to get you two together. If you want to date, go for it. I won't object. Unless." She pointed a finger at Travis. "You break her heart."

All heads swung his way.

"Me?" Travis stood.

"You ran off to Juilliard—" Emily pointed to the pair of us.

"But I always intended to go." Travis threw his napkin on the table and stalked into the kitchen.

Emily pouted. "It's a wonder he can walk with the stick up his—"

"I'll talk to him." I slid back my chair.

Emily wriggled closer to Jake. He placed his arm around her shoulders and drew her into his embrace. I sighed. I wanted what they had. An undeniable love. Affection. Companionship. Everything that came with it.

Would Travis be the one to give me everything?

I entered the kitchen, but it was empty. Alarm speared through my veins. Where did Travis go? I opened the back door and glimpsed his figure moving toward the driveway. Was Travis leaving? When he'd only just returned. Did he not experience the same feelings around me as I did him? My stomach clamped in a hard knot.

I needed to know because if he didn't, it was time I moved on with my life and stopped waiting for the impossible with Travis. No matter how good my memory of our kiss, and the length of my crush.

I ran after him. "Travis, wait."

Halfway across the street, I caught him. My hand landed on his arm and he turned around.

"Where are you going?"

"I needed air. I needed to think, and I wanted to sit under the lemon tree." He waved his arm toward my house.

"Come on, then." I let go of his arm and made my way to my house.

The sensor light flicked on and illuminated our path to the backyard. In the back garden sat the lemon tree with a string of sparkling fairy lights hanging in the branches.

The lemon tree.

The one we kissed under. Was Travis thinking of the kiss?

"This is new." He sat on the velvety yellow cushions of the daybed under the lemon tree and reclined until he looked up at the leaves of the tree.

"The day bed was the first thing I added when I purchased the house from Mom and Dad." I shuffled from foot to foot.

"I have so many memories under this lemon tree."

"Me too." I held a mountain of memories under the lemon tree, and the one that marked me forever was our kiss, but I wouldn't stand here and wish for him to kiss me again. "I'll leave you to your air and thinking."

"Claire." He sighed. "Sit down. We need to talk."

Talk?

It never went well when someone said they wanted to talk. My palms sweated. I perched on the edge of the daybed and waited for Travis to speak.

Travis closed his eyes. "You were so young."

I understood what he meant. Our kiss. Did it mean he thought of our kiss, too? A small spark of hope flared in my heart.

"Almost fifteen," I whispered.

"I was almost eighteen. I shouldn't have kissed you."

"But you did." I didn't regret it. Our kiss was beautiful and perfect.

He opened his eyes. "I did. And—"

"And then you ignored me." I folded my arms. My blood heated with the remembered anger. "Then you kissed your ex-girlfriend at school, where I saw you."

"I did it on purpose."

"You did?" I squeezed my fingers into fists. I could punch him. No one would see. It was only him and me out here.

He sat up and leaned forward. "I couldn't talk to you, I couldn't lie and tell you our kiss meant nothing, and I wanted you to be happy. I'd already applied and had been accepted to Juilliard. And you were so young..."

"I get it," I said, standing. He was too much that close. His lips were within kissing distance. Even with how stupid he was, I wanted to kiss him.

"Do you?" He stood with me.

I rolled my shoulders. I didn't. I wanted to, but my feelings for Travis would never change.

"Claire Bear," he whispered, taking my hands in his. "Last Christmas, coming home, seeing you again after all those years of avoiding you whenever I traveled home. I realized how wrong I was."

"Wrong?" I stared at his hands wrapped around mine. His pale skin clashed with my tanned fingers, but it was perfect. The feel, the connection, the rapid beat of my heart through my veins, with Travis touching me.

"I was wrong about all of it. You and me. The way I felt about you." He swallowed. "Still feel."

An owl hooted somewhere in the garden. I couldn't move. Didn't want to. Afraid I'd shatter the moment I'd longed for if I did.

Travis lifted his hands with mine wrapped inside them still. Slowly, he turned our hands over and placed a soft kiss on the inside of my wrist. Tingles raced up my arm. He pried open my fingers and placed butterfly kisses on my palms. I sighed with every emotion I held for Travis, had held for him for a long time. His gaze snapped to mine. A question lingered in his coffee-colored eyes.

I nodded my head. I forgave his stupidity. We were teenagers, after all, and maybe he was right, we were so young. Now we were adults, living in the same city, and nothing stopped us from seeing where our feelings for each other went.

Travis smiled. He stepped closer to me under the lemon tree.

Our lemon tree.

Gently, he drew me into his arms. Placed a hand on the side of my face and ran his thumb over my lips.

"I've dreamed of these lips," he whispered.

"No more dreaming." I threaded my fingers into his thick hair and tugged his head toward mine. "For either of us."

He pressed his delicious lips to mine.

If I'd considered him the best kisser ever with our first kiss, then this one...my legs turned to jelly, stars burst behind my eyelids, and my heart pounded inside my chest, full of emotion. So full of love and happiness.

Travis lifted his head. "I know you made the pumpkin pie."

"You do? How?" I asked, playing with his hair.

"Emily can't even reheat a frozen meal. I hope Jake can cook."

I laughed. "Who do you think helped with dinner?"

Travis laughed with me. "Why did you give up on your acting career?"

I shrugged. "I love my job as a teacher."

"You were always so good at school. I remember every play you acted in. Juliet was an outstanding performance."

"I don't know. It just didn't pan out for me, and I couldn't take the constant rejection."

"I hope you believe that I never wanted to reject you."

"You did what you thought you needed to." I glanced away.

"Hey." He turned my chin back toward him. "I've hated myself for a long time for what I did to you. I've spent a lot of time wishing I'd never known how good it was to kiss you in the first place. And I've wished for the day I could make it up to you."

"Yeah?"

"Claire Bear will you let me make it up to you?"

I tugged his head closer. Happiness ran through every inch of my body. "Yes."

Travis's gaze lit with hunger.

He kissed me again.

And again.

And again.

Each kiss was the best kiss.

Ever.

I forgave Travis because we'd been so young. His future was already waiting for him before we'd kissed. Maybe both our futures were. Somehow we ended up on the daybed curled in each other's arms and kissing like if our mouths separated then we'd die. His tongue stroked mine, and I never imagined us kissing as adults. It was way better than when we'd been teenagers. There'd been the quickness back then to our kiss that wasn't there now. Now, we lingered with every touch of our lips, every stroke of our tongues. Our hands joined the action.

That was all it took to send the kiss into more. Travis tore my dress from my body. Not literally, but he may as well have with how quickly he pulled the material over my head. I fumbled with his shirt buttons and gave up in frustration, pulling the fabric and popping the buttons from his shirt. The buttons pinged on the pavers but I didn't take no heed of the way we were quickly undressing each other.

We slammed back together. Our naked chests ignited sparks of lust and desire over my breasts and tight nipples. Travis groaned into our kiss, dragging his hands down my naked back. I straddled my legs over his hips and rolled them against the thick erection straining inside his pants.

"Claire."

"Yeah?"

"I want you so much it hurts."

I rolled my hips again enjoying the friction on my core. His hands dipped to the waistband of my thong and toyed with the strap.

"Can I take these off?"

"You're asking now after you've removed most of my clothes?" I asked, containing my laughter.

"Good point."

He flipped our positions so my back landed on the daybed and he kneeled between my spread knees. His gaze lit with a hunger that had my thighs trembling from just his look. Reverently, he slid his hands along the sensitive skin on the inside of my thighs, following the curve to my hips, he hooked my thong around his fingers and tugged it free from my legs.

"You're so beautiful."

"Says the man with his face on billboards."

He shrugged. "Part of the job. You should audition again. With your looks and skills, you'd be a star."

I scoffed.

"I'm serious, Claire. If it's what you want."

I sat forward and placed my hands on his zipper. "I want you. Does that count?"

"More than anything right now."

My fingers tugged the zipper down on his pants, and surprise of all surprises, Travis was commando. His cock sprang through his parted pants. I wrapped my hand around his length, shuddering at the sensation of his silky hard skin. I almost couldn't believe I was touching him so intimately.

At least Emily had given us her approval was the last thought in my mind before Travis's fingers slid over my quivering stomach and down to my damp core. As his fingers found the hard tip of my clit, I sucked in an aroused breath of longing. How many times had I dreamed of Travis this way? How many times had I thought it would never happen?

And here we were in my backyard of all places about to bring my dreams to life.

Travis shifted down making me lose the grip on his cock. His lips landed on my inner thigh before finding my core with his tongue. I almost shot off the daybed. The twinkling lights above me faded compared to the fireworks going off in my body. His hands clasped my hips and angled me so his mouth swallowed every drop of arousal seeping from my body. My legs quivered. He moaned against my sensitive flesh. The vibrations set my insides to a detonation point.

His lips disappeared from my body. I whined in the agony of the almost ecstasy he'd denied me.

"We're coming together."

I lay on the daybed gasping for breath but nodding. Together sounded right. We'd waited this long to be together, why shouldn't we do everything together?

He slid his hand into his pocket, took out his wallet, and then a condom. Thank the heavens for him being prepared. I don't think my legs would work to walk inside the house to get the condoms in my bedroom. He rolled the protection onto his straining cock.

"Seeing you like that..." He shook his head. "You undo me."

I crooked my finger at him. He shook his head as his hands landed on my body again. With a firm push of his hands, he rolled me over and dragged my hips into the air.

"Out of all the things I fantasized about the most, it was your ass."

I giggled. Who knew Travis was an ass man. And I was always calling him an ass.

My laughter died the second the flared head of his cock brushed against my slick entrance. He slid into me so slowly that I thought he might change his mind about doing this with me, but when he'd landed balls deep inside me, he leaned forward and brushed a tender kiss against the side of my neck.

"Claire Bear," he whispered.

I shivered. So many emotions filled those two words. His fingers slid to my front and stroked my clit. Keeping his chest against my back, he rocked his hips back and thrust forward. Every nerve ending in my body built with the anticipation for him to do it again. He did. My legs trembled. Every breath filled with the need for more. For Travis.

"Travis," I moaned his name.

He picked up his pace. Thrusting in a rhythm that was perfect with the strumming of his fingers. There was only Travis. Only him making me feel so good. So happy. Each slide of his cock drew me closer to the peak as my inner muscles clamped. His fingers toyed with my clit until sparks of pleasure danced over every inch of my skin. Before I knew it, the orgasm was on me, making my inner muscles spasm against his cock. His fingers dragged the pulsating release out until my breath no longer worked and then Travis came deep inside me and I'd never felt more complete than in this moment.

As though we'd sealed our future together forever.

After my breathing returned to normal, as well as Travis's who seemed to be as ragged as mine, he slid from my body making my insides weep at the loss. But Travis picked me up before I let myself fall face-first on the mattress. He sat me on his lap, brushed my hair back from my face, and kissed me so tenderly that tears welled at the corner of my eyes.

"I love you, Claire Bear."

Sucking in a shuddering breath, I said, "I love you, too."

I snuggled closer to his chest. He stroked my back in soothing circles.

"Now what?" I asked.

Travis laughed. "Now we do that all over again."

I laughed. "That wasn't what I meant."

"Could have fooled me," he said. "You've been lusting after my cock forever."

"Ass." I laughed even harder.

"Best Thanksgiving ever."

"I'll say," I said, grinning. "Today is lust giving from now on."

"I'll give you lust." Travis stood with me in his arms forgetting his pants were still wrapped around his thighs as he tried to walk and stumbled. We ended up back on the day bed.

"Guess we're stuck here," I teased, looking up into the smiling face of the man I'd loved for longer than I'd care to admit to.

"I couldn't think of anywhere else I'd rather be stuck than here with you."

Could I smile any bigger? Be any happier? As we lay side by side tangled in limbs gazing at the twinkling lights, I almost couldn't believe this was real.

"Pinch me," I said.

"I'll never hurt you again," Travis said.

My heart swelled with certainty this was it for Travis and me. Our future was ours together.

Afterword

Thank you for reading The Lust Giving.
Did you love my story?
Review it!

A reader who writes a review for a book is a tremendous gift to the author. It lets me know that someone read my book and enjoyed the story enough to tell me. If you enjoyed this book, please leave a review. I'd be forever grateful.

Acknowledgments

First, thank you to my family for putting up with me disappearing into the world of books. To Belinda, thank you for encouraging me to write again after I lost everything in a computer crash. Remember to back up! A lot of work goes into creating a story, and I'm always thankful for the support of my online writing buddies, beta readers, and fellow authors, Immy for always making me smile, Tammy for believing in me from the start, Karen for being willing to read any level of heat I write. Cassie for her hand holding. Lana for her invaluable knowledge. Also, my fabulous beta reader Erica and her help with US English. The biggest thank you goes to my 'twin' Dannielle, who is the best critique partner, cheerleader, and sounding board ever, and is forever fixing my comma errors, sorry Dannielle I'm afraid you're stuck with them and me. Finally thank you to all you romance readers. You are my tribe.

About Author

Helen Walton is a tea drinking, chocoholic, romance writer. Stories are her obsession. She adores creating sensual romances containing a sprinkling of humor and the all-important happy ending. She lives in South Australia with her family, and menagerie of quirky animals where they all take her away from her book world and demand to be fed. Lucky for them, she enjoys cooking but prefers baking.

Sign up for my newsletter for exclusive content.

https://www.helenwaltonauthor.com/newsletter
Visit my website

https://www.helenwaltonauthor.com/

Follow me

bookbub.com/profile/helen-walton

facebook.com/Helen-Walton-Author-1 03496667706602/

goodreads.com/author/show/20249188 .Helen_Walton

instagram.com/helen.walton.author

tiktok.com/@helen.walton.author

HELEN WALTON

Also By

FANTASY AND PARANORMAL ROMANCE
Summer Court

Fae's Song

Fae's Wolf

Fae's Alpha

Fae's Heart

Fae's Witch

HELEN WALTON

Anthologies

Reluctant Bride

Alpha Male

www.ingramcontent.com/pod-product-compliance
Lightning Source LLC
Chambersburg PA
CBHW030419120726
47904CB00007B/2341